Monsters Love Underpants

To Dr. M. J. Smith, with thanks ~ C. F.

For Doreen and family, with love ~ B. C.

Originally published in Great Britain in 2014 by Simon and Schuster UK, Ltd.

ISBN 978-0-545-91497-0

12 11 10 9 8 7 6 5 4 3 2   15 16 17 18 19 20/0

Printed in the U.S.A.   08

This edition first printing, September 2015

Designed by Karina Granda

Monsters Love Underpants

ILLUSTRATED BY
Ben Cort

CLAIRE FREEDMAN

SCHOLASTIC INC.

Monsters think it's MONSTER fun,

   to creep around, all scary!

But there's something they love even MORE,

   than looking mean and hairy!

Monsters all LOVE underpants,
    and think pants are fun-tastic.
They like all patterns, shapes, and styles,
    and twanging pants elastic!

Some prowl through dingy dungeons: "Oooooow!"
You hear them howling, loudly.
CREAK! One finds squeaky armour pants,
and clanks around SO proudly!

Drool monsters from the steamy swamp,
fill pants with gooey slime.
But, OOOOPS! Their pants get slippery,
and slide down all the time!

Wild, woolly mountain monsters
make explorers faint with fright!
CLOMP! They snatch their frozen pants,
then run off in the night!

At the bottom of the ocean,
    a pirate ship now rests.
Where sea monsters wear pants with jewels
    they've pinched from treasure chests!

The spiky, spooky, space monsters
all wave and roar, "Hooray!"
When out from blackest, deepest space,
bright bloomers float their way!

It's not the sand inside his pants
    that makes this monster twitchy.
His underpants are way too small.
"I wish they weren't so itchy!"

It's Saturday—their Disco Night.

They wear pants bold and brave.

The password (sshh!) is WOBBLY PANTS,

to get inside the cave.

The monsters show their pants off
as they dance the Monster Bop.
Their pants-clad bottoms jig and jive,
till someone yells out, "STOP!"

"It's almost daylight! Quick, back home . . .
we can't risk being spotted!
For no one will be scared of us
in pants all striped and dotted!"

So if you hear strange scuffles
    from beneath your bed—
    beware!
You might just catch a monster
    trying on YOUR
    snazzy pair!